THE
BLUE
BUTTERFLY

by Ned O'Gorman
Pictures by Thomas di Grazia

HARPER & ROW, PUBLISHERS
New York, Evanston, San Francisco, London

THE BLUE BUTTERFLY

FIRST EDITION

CONTENTS

Part One

THE BLUE BUTTERFLY:

THE FIRST ADVENTURE

On a day just like this a Blue Butterfly climbed a mountain and sat inside a glass box. When he had settled down to a silver dish filled with milk and honey, a Cow, tired of eating daffodils and oats, took a swim in a pool beside his pasture. The Blue Butterfly looked down from the top of his mountain, and saw the Cow, and said to himself, "Enough of this lazy day. I want to swim."

So the Blue Butterfly flew down and fluttered about the edge of the pool. To tell the truth he was afraid of water. The Cow looked up and brushed away the water from his eyes with his tail, and said, "Come in. Sit on my ear and swim."

And so they did. When they had enough of water, they went to the bank and had a lunch of green apples, white cheese, hazelnuts and raisins and cucumbers.

In the forest, beyond the pasture and beyond the mountain, a Lion and three lonely Birds of Paradise were hot. Their waterfall had dried up, and there was no place to swim.

The Lion grumbled, ROAR RRRRRR, SUM ZUN DUM DEE, RUMBLE SQUISH RISHO LIMP LIND ING.

The Birds of Paradise said to each other, RUCK DINGLE DINGLE FILT, OOOO RINDK SUN DUM PLAP.

And they took a journey over the mountain, across the pasture to the Cow's pool, and said to the Cow and Butterfly—who offered them a piece of cucumber, for that was all that was left—"We are hot. May we swim?"

"Oh, my, yes, you may," the Butterfly and the Cow said at once.

And the Butterfly, the Cow, the Lion and the three Birds of Paradise went for a swim.

They swam like this:

The Butterfly on the Cow's ear.
The Birds of Paradise on the Lion's head.

When they had enough of the cool water, they all decided to go to see some children.

The Town of Children was across a sea, and on the edge of the sea was an iceberg. They all climbed upon it, and the Lion stood in the middle of the iceberg. The wind caught in his mane like a sail, and they drifted off toward the children.

The children met them on the bank of a vegetable and flower garden; and the children rang bells, shot off fireworks, sang the songs of dreams, and served them banana cakes, ice-

5

cream popcorn, maple-syrup candy canes and lemon-covered chocolate cookies. The children said, "Let's take a swim in the pool near the carrots and tulips."

This is how they swam:

> *The Butterfly on the Birds of Paradise—*
> *flitting from one to another, resting*
> *on their crests.*
> *The Lion and the Cow carried the children,*
> *on their heads, on their backs,*
> *and on their tails.*

The children were:

BRILLIANT—*A black girl with an ivory band around her wrist.*

DROUSELLA—*A girl from Asia with a red bead on her chin and a golden bird hanging from one ear.*

MOUSHOUBIE—*A boy from Egypt who lived in a tent shaped like the sun.*

HEPSIBIA—*A white boy with green eyes.*

Then when they had finished in the water, they climbed back on the bank of the pool and had tea, of root beer in green glasses, cotton candy on pussy-willow stalks, and stuffed apples with blue berries and orange slices inside.

Then they heard a loud, terrible noise in the distance, and out of a hill came a train, and it stopped right beside them on the bank of the pool. "Get on me," the train seemed to say. And on they all got and went on a journey through the world, stopping now and then to read, sleep, eat, dream of home, sing, and thank each other for being so happy.

Then on an afternoon when the train had taken them to the Land of the Silver Chimneys and the Green Shells, the Blue Butterfly said,

"I must go back to my mountain. I miss it and don't want to stay here anymore."

Everyone was lonely, and they all decided to return home. The Birds of Paradise to their Rainbow Trees, the Lion to his black rock cave, the children to their rooms and to their own windows. ("We have been looking out of windows at things we didn't know for too long," Brilliant thought.) And the Butterfly to his glass box on the mountaintop.

*   *   *

The trip to see the children was fun, but now it was over. The mountaintop was lonely. The Cow was away in another pasture over the hills.

"So," the Blue Butterfly thought, "why not take a trip?" Yes, that was an idea. "But where to? To the zoo?" No, he'd been there and knew everyone. He missed Brilliant, Drousella, Moushoubie, and Hepsibia. "What about a trip to the seaside? No. A lot of wind there and sand. The wind tosses me around and the sand weighs down my wings."

10

He went to sleep. The mountaintop was so high that it was always in the sun, and when he woke up, he just *had* to go away. "I'll visit Brilliant. Yes I will. She lives in Africa. I will like it there."

So the Blue Butterfly packed a fan to keep himself cool in the forests, a mirror to look behind to see what had happened, and a wooden fork.

He locked the glass box, put the key on a hook outside, and went on his way.

He climbed higher than the mountain. The land below was clear and bright as a new flower garden in April. He sang and tumbled in the thin, cool air. When he flew ten hours, he thought it was time for bed, and he looked down for a place to sleep and saw a doorway in a forest. It was made of ivory and leaves. Animals, letters, flowers and numbers were carved in the ivory. Over the door was a stone arch and in the doorway, looking up into the sky, was his friend Brilliant.

"Oh, my," she shouted loud. "There he is, my

friend the Blue Butterfly. Just little as a seed in the sky, but it is *him*." And down the Blue Butterfly came.

"Hello. I love you. I missed you. But oh, I am hungry." And they both sat down in the doorway and had lunch of yellow fish soup, nut cake, leopard meat fried in onions, and an ice-cold forest juice.

They talked of this and that, and through the doorway the Blue Butterfly saw the world Brilliant lived in: the castle of the King; the children playing ball; the cars they drove in the forest; the vegetables they ate; and a river that flowed past the doorway, dancing in and out of the light, now dark, now so sparkling that the Blue Butterfly shut his wings tight (for butterflies see the world through their wings); and in a cove of wild flowers sat the King.

"Come here," he said to the Blue Butterfly, and the Blue Butterfly flew and sat on the edge of his wrist.

"Yes," he said, "what do you want?"

"Oh, nothing," said the King. "Just, how are you? are you happy? and stay as long as you like."

The Blue Butterfly flew back to the doorway and spent the day with Brilliant, running, wondering, and looking.

At eight o'clock Brilliant went to sleep. And the Butterfly did too, on the top of a flower so blue, that if you looked at it, you would have to look hard to see the Blue Butterfly asleep.

*   *   *

The Blue Butterfly spent a week with Brilliant and then said, when they were swimming in the sparkling river, "I must be off. Soon my friend the Cow will come back to his pasture, and I want to greet him when he returns. But I must make one more visit before I go home. Hepsibia lives in a city. It is in America somewhere. Good-bye, Brilliant. Good-bye, King."

He flew to the edge of a wheat field and met a Tortoise sleeping between two sunflowers.

"America is across this field. Will you carry me there?" The Tortoise said he would, and the Blue Butterfly climbed on his back, and in a day they were on a hill overlooking the city.

It looked very peculiar. Very crowded, and it took the Blue Butterfly some time to find where Hepsibia lived. Doors doors doors doors. But no door he saw would be the kind of door Hepsibia would sit in.

And just when he was ready to go home he saw a bright-yellow door made of wood. Two cats and a horse played in front of it on a little pasture. A motor roared in the air and hurt the Blue Butterfly's tiny legs. (Butterflies hear the world through their legs.) Hepsibia sat there reading a newspaper. CRUSH CRUSH BAN SMASH SCREECH.

The Blue Butterfly sat on his ear, and Hepsibia knew who was sitting there without looking. "Hello. How are you? I have missed you. Are you hungry?"

"No. I have just come from a trip across a

15

beautiful field, and I ate barley and the cherry blossom."

"Sit down with me," Hepsibia said, "and look at what is going on here in the city."

The Blue Butterfly did not like what he saw. A man ran down a dark street, and a car chased him. "Hepsibia was happier," the Blue Butterfly thought, "when the other children were with him, and they could swim in the pool near the carrots and tulips."

"I am going back home," the Blue Butterfly said. "I don't like it here."

"I don't either," said Hepsibia, and he packed a paper bag with a drum and drumsticks, a paintbrush and some paints (for he was an artist) and went with the Blue Butterfly as far as a valley.

"You know," said the Blue Butterfly, who was getting used to traveling now and wanted to go on a little more, "Drousella lives across this valley. Can you make out a silver and orange dot on the top of that hill? Well, there she is. Let's go."

Hepsibia said, "No. Not now. It is such a lovely view. I want to sit down and paint it."

The Butterfly said okay, and Hepsibia took out his brush and paints and took a piece of bark off a tree, flattened it out, and began to paint.

It was a beautiful picture although the Blue Butterfly couldn't quite make out what Hepsibia had drawn.

"I'm finished now. Let's go."

"Okay," said the Blue Butterfly, and they went slowly across the valley.

It was very quiet, that valley. There were no people there, no animals, no noises. Just grass and colored stones. Hepsibia wanted to draw everything he saw, but the Blue Butterfly said that they must get to Drousella before it got dark.

The silver and orange dot came closer and closer, and soon they saw what it was. A door in the middle of a rice field. The door was silver, and over it was a bell tower with ten orange bells ringing.

Drousella sat in the doorway, weaving a carpet from a ball of colored silk.

*   *   *

"First we must dance," said Hepsibia.

Drousella was so happy to see the Blue Butterfly that she dropped her ball of colored silk, and it rolled down through the rice field.

Hepsibia took out his drum and drumsticks, the Blue Butterfly flapped his wings together, and the ten orange bells played an Asian tune. They all danced in circles, triangles, and just however they pleased.

Then they sat down and looked at one another.

"You know," said Drousella, "there is a mountain over there made of honeysuckle vines and parrot nests, and at the top there must be a wonderful thing because every night a light flashes from the sky and a bell rings. Let's climb that mountain."

And up they went:

First the Blue Butterfly,
then Drousella, carrying her ball of silk,
and behind (to catch her if she fell)
Hepsibia, playing a tune on his drum.

It was an easy climb. They hung on the honeysuckle vines, and the parrots came out now and then to say, "Good luck."

The higher they climbed, the lower the sun set. And finally, just before it disappeared, the top of the mountain flashed, and they heard the tinkling of a bell. The Blue Butterfly reached the top first, and Hepsibia and Drousella heard him laugh. Well, they had never heard a Butter-fly laugh, and they climbed faster to see what was going on.

And there they saw the Blue Butterfly, laughing and flying around in his glass box. For what Drousella had seen flashing in the dusk was the Blue Butterfly's house, and the bell she heard was the key clinking against it in the wind.

21

"Well," said the Blue Butterfly, "that was a surprise. You know, I never explored that side of the mountain." And Hepsibia took out his paint and painted the Blue Butterfly laughing. And Drousella began weaving a rug of a Blue Butterfly inside a glass box on the top of a mountain, and in the distance she wove her silver doorway, the orange bells and the rice fields.

Part Two

THE BLUE BUTTERFLY

AND THE GREEN PERIWINKLE

OVERCOME DIFFICULTIES

In that part of the ocean near the sands where seaweed grows on small rocks and where no sharks or whales go—it is shallow there, and they need deep water—there lived a Green Periwinkle who was happy most of the time.

Today he began to feel unhappy.

"I wonder why? I have been happy every day till now. But today isn't like other days."

So the day began. The Green Periwinkle was sleeping under a pink, blue, black and lavender rock. The seaweed growing on it floated upward, and the tops turned gold when the sun slid up over the cliff the Periwinkle saw every day when the tide went out.

He lived under water most of the time.

He had never seen the cliff close enough to know what it felt like, nor had he ever felt the sand on his feet nor the heat of the shells on his face. Between his shoal and the cliff was a secret and mysterious land.

"I think I know why I am unhappy. I want to climb up that thing out there." (He didn't know it was a cliff.) "I want to see where the sun comes from."

"Oh, I'll take you along with me," said someone who had landed on the top of the Periwinkle's shell.

"Who are you? I can't see you."

"I am the Blue Butterfly, and I saw you from the cliff over there, and you looked unhappy. I thought you'd like to take a trip. I'm going to the Village and need someone to talk to."

"I'll go along," said the Green Periwinkle, "and so *that's* what the sun slides over in the morning—a 'cliff.' That's a good name. Cliff, cliff, cliff."

"Hang on my wing and we'll fly to the shore. I can't take you longer than that. You look very heavy."

"My, that is a good feeling," said the Green Periwinkle as he made his way across the sand. "It certainly isn't 'wet.' What is that feeling?"

"That," said the Blue Butterfly, "is 'dry.'"

"And what is this I feel on my back, like a prickly chip of shell but deeper inside me? That surely isn't 'cold.'"

"That," said the Blue Butterfly, "is 'hot.'"

"Well, the shore is full of surprises, and oh my, oh my, I guess this is 'cliff,'" he said as he came up against a high place he couldn't see over or climb up.

It was a blue clay cliff and very slippery. But coming down the cliff from the top was a clear stream of rainwater. "Now," said the Blue Butterfly, "I think if you try, you can get up to the top of the cliff by moving up that stream."

"Oh no," said the Periwinkle. "I never move off my rock. How do you think I could ever climb up a slippery stream of water?"

"If you don't, you'll never see the Village or the church or the band or the marketplace. Try, or go back to the ocean."

And the Periwinkle tried. He slipped back down on the dry, hot sand ten times and was pretty tired; but he looked up and saw the Blue Butterfly looking down at him, and he held his breath and tried hard and got to the top, and rested there an hour to get his breath. (Periwinkles have very little bodies and very little breath.)

The trip into the Village was great fun. The Butterfly pointed out these things to the Periwinkle: grass, stones (dry and very dull to the Periwinkle's eye, for he'd been used to underwater rocks that are like rainbows), beetles, snakes, cows and an eagle feather that had fallen from the sky into a rosebush. He didn't bother about cars because when the Periwinkle saw one, he got so frightened that the Butterfly changed their way to the Village from along the road to across the fields. "I don't want to know what that is," he told the Blue Butterfly when he heard a car coming.

29

The Periwinkle tried to remember every-thing, but he remembered only the snakes be-cause the snakes seemed to him like something he once saw in the shoal.

"It was probably an eel," said the Blue Butter-fly.

The Village was in a valley. There was a garden in the middle of it with a hammock, a swing, a soda fountain and a bandstand. There was a fountain too; but it had gone dry, and everyone had to get their water from a well in the churchyard.

A band was playing when they got to the garden, and they listened for a while, but the Periwinkle said it was too loud. "All I've ever heard is waves and seaweed in the undertow. I don't like that 'band'—especially that terrible sound from those two things that man hits to-gether."

"Those are cymbals."

"I don't like cymbals and besides I'm thirsty. There's no water in the fountain. What do we do?"

They went to the churchyard and climbed up on the rim of the well, and that was a problem right there that could prove hard to solve. The Periwinkle got into the bucket, and the Blue Butterfly tried to lower the bucket into the well, but that didn't work because the Blue Butterfly couldn't move the winch. So they waited for someone to come along. A lady did, with a donkey, five children, a parrot, and a gold pin in her hair. The Periwinkle got on the Butterfly's wing, stepped out onto the rim of the bucket, got a free ride into the well and drank up some water.

Then they went to the marketplace.

"That is a cantaloupe. That is a pineapple. Those are vegetables: cucumbers, onions, persimmons (someone made a mistake and put one in with the onions) and potatoes."

"What does a pineapple taste like?"

"Well," said the Blue Butterfly, "it's sweet."

"What is 'sweet'?"

"It's not salty. But come on, we'll taste it."

31

The trouble there was that neither of them knew how to get inside the hard outside of the pineapple. "I'll push it over," said the Periwinkle. "I'm pretty strong if I'm really curious." And he pushed and pushed and finally, when he was ready to faint away, the pineapple fell onto the stone floor of the market and *squish*, *swuash* there it was all open; and in the middle of it, swimming around and slurping, were the Periwinkle and the Butterfly.

"It's better than salt, this 'sweet,' although I think I'd miss my seaweed juice after a while. Where do you live, Butterfly? I'd like to see your house."

"I've been living a bit on the top of a church on a silver-arrow weather vane. I can see everything from there, and it is cool. Come on with me, and we'll see if you can get up there."

That *was* a difficulty to overcome.

They got into church, and the Blue Butterfly said it might be okay to climb up the stairs to the choir loft, and then up the tiny curving stair to the tower, and then outside on the narrow

34

wooden railing where the Blue Butterfly would carry the Periwinkle to the weather vane, on his wings.

When they got to the railing, a wind had skipped up over the cliff down the hills into the valley. But the Butterfly was so used to quiet weather he did not notice it coming up toward him from the garden, the marketplace and the well. Just as they had started up through the air a little wind hit them, the Blue Butterfly lost his balance, and they tumbled out of control toward the marketplace. "Hold on, hold on," said the Blue Butterfly, but he was really scared, and the Periwinkle thought that he was surely going to bash his shell up on the cantaloupe they were falling toward. Blue Butterfly beat his wings like a wild eagle, and just as they were going to hit the earth he made one gigantic last flap and mounted the wind, and–wonder of wonder–the wind that had cast him down carried him up to the weather vane.

"Life over the cliff is hard, isn't it?" said the Periwinkle. "Let's just sit here a bit."

35

The weather vane turned slowly in the warm, cantaloupe–pineapple–well-water air, and the Periwinkle saw all the world—and one part of it that made him lonely all over again. For there in the distance were his shoal and his rocks, green and blue, and the sunlight on them like a thin golden shell. "I am lonely. I think I want to go back now."

And together they returned to the edge of the cliff. By then the Periwinkle had grown used to the dry world and got along quite well by himself. They slid down the stream in the blue clay and found themselves a little farther away from the Periwinkle's shoal than they had figured on. In front of them, at the roof of the cliff, was a sand dune. They started to climb it.

When the Blue Butterfly got near the top, he exploded with a *flitter flattery rishymythy* of wings and said, "Oh my, it snowed while we were away, and a yellow bird got stuck on top of a pile of snow." For true to say and strange to say, on the other side of the sand dune they saw a white mountain and a yellow bird ker-plunk on the top.

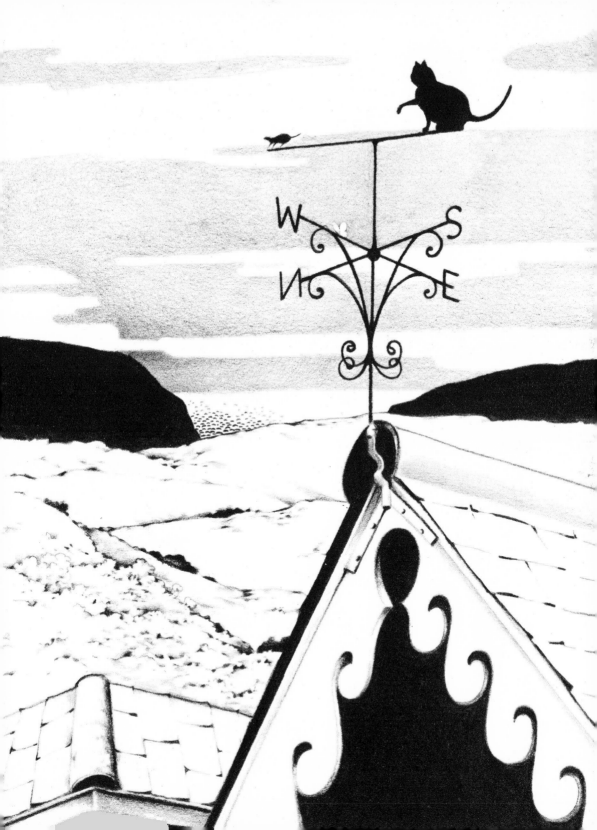

The Blue Butterfly had to tell the Periwinkle about snow, and he was sure he didn't understand at all. "It is sort of like sand but colder and lighter, and turns into water when the sun touches it."

"How could anything turn into water," said the Periwinkle, "when I know and you know perfectly well that everything *is* water?"

When they got to the top of the sand dune, they carefully stepped on top of the snow hill and climbed to the bird and poked it. It didn't move at all. "Maybe he is dead of the cold," said the Blue Butterfly. But he was warm, and when the Periwinkle poked it with the sharp end of his shell it crinkled like straw.

"It is not a real bird at all. It's straw," said the Blue Butterfly. "His eyes are bits of green cloth. But this snow isn't much either. I can't slide on it at all, and oh, would you look at *that*," he said to the Periwinkle, who was finding it hard to keep upright on the snow hill.

Both of them peered over the edge of the hill and looked into their own faces, for the snow hill wasn't a snow hill at all. It was a beautiful white-linen bonnet of a girl with red hair, who

38

sat on the sand looking at herself in a mirror. When she saw the Butterfly and the Periwinkle looking at her through the mirror, she turned her head quickly and bumped them off onto the sand, where they stayed a while because they had fallen rather a long way.

"Well, let's be off. Come on," the Blue Butterfly said, "and take hold of my wing, and I'll lead you back home."

"No, thank you," said the Periwinkle. "I'm okay. I can get on by myself," and off he went bravely into the dark toward the waves that came ("like black cymbals," he thought) in from the sea to his shoal.

The Blue Butterfly flew up into the air and came to rest on the bonnet of the red-haired girl, who carried him up the cliff and back to the Village, where he spent the night on the arrow weather vane that floated in his dreams toward the moon.

Part Three

THE BLUE BUTTERFLY,

THE ORANGE ORANGUTAN, AND

THE GREY AND LIGHT-BLACK SPIDER

WITH THIRTEEN LEGS

GREET MOUSHOUBIE

The Blue Butterfly had settled in quite comfortably in his glass box. After the adventures with the children and the Periwinkle, he decided it was time to rest a little.

And so he did, but nervously. He loved to go here and there and see the different, beautiful and odd things in the world.

"I will get up tomorrow morning," he said to himself one day, "and go out and do some discovering." He went to bed early. Beside his bed he put a large green leaf with cucumber bread and ten yellow seeds wrapped up inside. He especially liked to chew the seeds when he felt lonely on his journeys.

But he slept so well that he got up at ten o'clock, not at five o'clock as he had planned. (The Blue Butterfly never owned a clock. He never worried about *when* to do anything—"I just *do* things," he told someone who asked him why he didn't own a clock or even a sundial.)

He looked out at the mountains. The sun rose over the hill behind the pasture, a large orange ball slowly floating up out of the blue sky.

He thought, "It certainly is a beautiful sun, but I don't remember it looking quite so rough and hairy, and I do think it is making a sound."

Gmpdd ĝlr ĝlr rtuim ktrum rish.

"And for goodness sake, it's got eyes and a nose and a mouth."

He knew then it wasn't the sun, but what it was he didn't know. (Had he a sundial, he would have known that it wasn't the sun. It had risen four hours ago.) He got up and pushed open the glass front door, the key tinkled, and he flew toward the hill to get a better look.

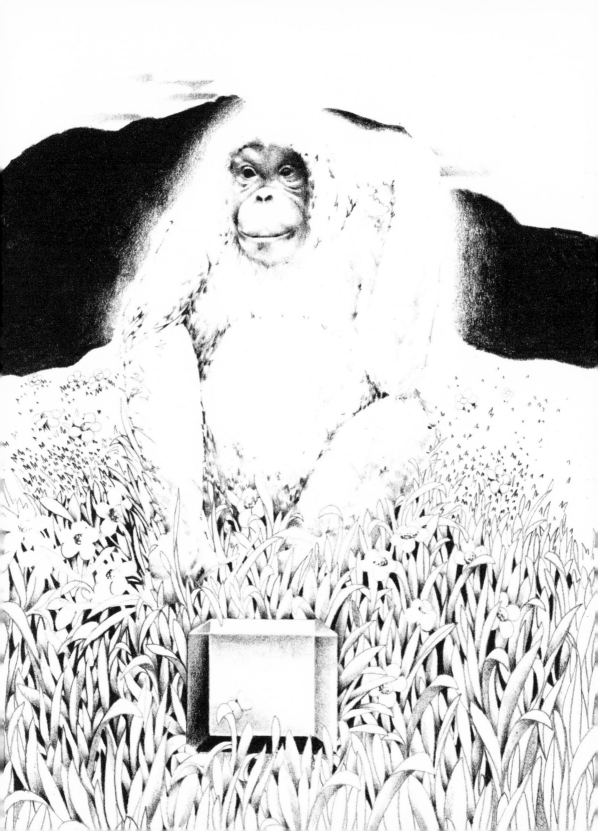

"What are you? and what is your name? and are you planning to stay here awhile? because I am lonely and want to talk to someone."

The Yellow Thing (it was really more orange than yellow) looked around to see who was talking, and when it saw the Blue Butterfly dancing around its head, it said, "I am the Orange Orangutan from Sumatra, and I will stay as long as you like. I've just come from the forest. I had a fight with a friend about antelopes and war and wanted to get away. I think I'd like to go down that hill and see what's in that field over there. There is something funny and pointed with a hole in the middle of it, and I am curious."

The Blue Butterfly went back to get his green leaf, and the Orange Orangutan and his small blue friend started off.

"You certainly are big. I just know children and a small Green Periwinkle. How much do you weigh? Are you hungry? I don't have much, but here's a yellow seed. It is very good and makes you feel strong and amusing."

45

"I weigh five-hundred pounds. I eat very little. When I stand up and put my arms over my head to stretch out for an apple on a tree or something, I am eight feet tall. I am a peculiar orangutan; most orangutans eat a lot. That seed is good. What is it?"

"I don't know," said the Blue Butterfly. "A hummingbird brought them to me and said he liked them."

And then they came to the Field in the Distance. In the middle of it—it was a hot, bright-white, flat place of flying sands—was the largest thing the Blue Butterfly ever saw.

"You know about large things, what is that?" he asked the Orangutan.

"I think that is a pyramid. It is a place they put old and dead kings when the world had kings. They say that in the middle of it is a room filled with gold and jewels."

"Let's go," said the Blue Butterfly. Some of the chunks of marble had been taken out of the side of the Pyramid, and up about one-hundred

46

feet was a hole going inside. The Orangutan and the Blue Butterfly started up a stone stair. It was very dark.

"I can barely move," said the Orangutan. "I am far too big for this narrow stair, but I'll make it."

"Here's another seed. It'll make you feel thinner." The Blue Butterfly got up quite easily. The Orangutan could see him ahead. The Blue Butterfly had some white lines on his wings that caught whatever light there was in the Pyramid. (A little came squeaking up from the outside through the hole they came through.)

But both of them were a little edgy. Now and then a bat brushed past them, and they saw a snake slithering overhead, and a funny shadow jumped back and forth on the walls along the stair.

"What will we do when we get where we're going?" asked the Orangutan.

"Oh, we'll just look around at the gold and jewels and go back down again."

When they had climbed about five minutes, they came to a square, black stone room. There was a little light in it, but they couldn't find where it came from. (The Blue Butterfly thought it had been there a long time.)

"Where's all the gold and jewels?" asked the Orangutan. "There's nothing here but the room, walls, a damp floor and that shadow hopping across the ceiling."

"Someone must have come here before us and taken them away. I think it was bandits."

"Perhaps they're in the room now, waiting for us," said the Orangutan. "Do you think they'd take us away?"

"Of course not," said the Blue Butterfly. "We're not worth much, and bandits take things they can sell. No one would buy us."

When they got outside again (the jumping shadow and the funny light had followed them down the stairs and disappeared just before they got outside), they went across the desert and came to a river. There was a green hedge along one side of it, and on the hedge were purple and white cakes and berries. "Let's eat them," said the Blue Butterfly, and they swam across and sat down in the shade of the hedge and ate.

"Put the berries on this piece of cucumber bread: one slice on top, one slice underneath. We call that a sandwich in Sumatra."

The Orangutan said suddenly, "There is something climbing up my cheek. I can feel it, and I wonder, Blue Butterfly, if you'd be so kind and look there and see what it is."

"A spider. A very small spider with thirteen legs, and in the middle of all the legs is a body, grey and light-black, with two eyes, a nose and a mouth."

The Orangutan lifted up his orange paw to brush it away, but the Butterfly said not to because he'd kill the spider if he did. The spider climbed on the Blue Butterfly's wing and got safely back on the ground again.

"Whew," said the Grey and Light-Black Spider with Thirteen Legs, "that was a blunder, getting stuck on an orangutan's cheek. I was

coming down from a tree on a string we spiders spin from out of our tummies, and suddenly I was waylaid on that fellow's face."

The three of them—the Blue Butterfly, the Orange Orangutan and the Grey and Light-Black Spider with Thirteen Legs—found out they liked each other, and they went on their way to discover things.

*   *   *

When the sun was ready to set and they were tired, they came to a canyon. It was very deep, so deep that they could not see the bottom. They heard a river and thought they could see some trees and a cornfield sparkle in the light below, but they didn't want to go down. They wanted to go across to the other side of the canyon, where they saw some eggs, lemonade and three bunches of grapes on a stone table.

"I don't have a big appetite, but those yellow seeds and a cucumber and berry sandwich are really not enough for me," said the Orangutan.

They looked for a way to cross. The Blue Butterfly could fly, but then he'd have to leave his friends. That would never do.

They went a little way along the edge. The canyon turned sharply, and there, around the corner, they saw an Iron and Wooden Bridge going from their side of the canyon to the other.

The Bridge was held into the ground, on each side of the canyon, by gigantic marble pillars. It was a wooden bridge, and the sides of it were iron fences. Whoever had made the fences painted them scarlet, yellow, royal purple and white; and they had bent the metal into the shapes of famous things—jumping shadows, pyramids, stars, moons, clowns, dreams, Indians, weather vanes, turtles, kites, children, waves, hoops and bandits. The wood was black, and it was laid down in wide planks held together by brass clamps. It seemed very strong; and the Orange Orangutan, the Grey and Light-Black Spider with Thirteen Legs and the Blue Butterfly crossed over to the stone table.

They ate the eggs raw and put the grapes into the lemonade. They soaked up the last bit of the lemonade with a piece of cucumber bread and went to sleep.

*　　*　　*

In the morning they were very happy. They started off into the day, wondering what they would see next and what beautiful and curious thing would be waiting around the corner. They passed through rain forests and under stone arches carved out of black rock. They climbed hills and looked down into cities and villages. Once they saw a battle going on, and the Spider cried when he saw people and houses falling down in a clatter of guns and screaming.

"I hope there are no spiders down there. They aren't very strong, and they are not at all partial to noise."

At about noon the sun got very bright, and they smelled salt and fishes in the air. They had been pushing through some high grass for a long time; and when they were sure they were

55

lost, they saw a white cloth floating against the sky, and then four more white cloths; and when they had pushed the grass away once more, they saw that the cloths were sails and under the sails was a sailing ship made of brown and red timber with shining copper and silver fittings. The ship had come to anchor in a cove of the bluest water. ("It is as blue as your wings," said the Orangutan to the Blue Butterfly.) A plank went from the deck to the shore; and standing at the foot of the plank were Brilliant, Drousella, Hepsibia and a dark boy with long black hair and gold rings in his ears. A girl with red hair and a white straw hat, looking at herself in a mirror, held the Green Periwinkle in her hand. They said hello and sang a song and danced a little.

"We're sailing away in a minute or two," someone said. "We waited for you, and you came. Come along."

They all went up the plank—the Orange Orangutan and the Grey and Light-Black Spider with Thirteen Legs coming last.

"I'm Moushoubie," said the boy with the gold rings in his ears. "I come from Egypt, and I live in a tent shaped like the sun." He pulled up the plank and welcomed everyone aboard. "We're off to the Arctic Circle and then to the Nile and Katmandu. This is my boat. It is called *The Good Ship of the Friendly Winds and Secret Places.*"

The Blue Butterfly said thank you, and the Ship sailed away toward adventure and the beautiful, odd and curious things of this world.

But toward midnight, high on the tallest sail, where he was sleeping, the Blue Butterfly woke up to see the Ship pass a mountain, and on the top of it was a glass box and the sound of a bell came out over the sea.

"I must go back. That is my house; that is where I dream. That is where adventure begins." And quietly as a moonbeam he flew away and spent the night watching for the coming of the day.

57

Format by Gloria Bressler
Set in 14 pt. Bookman
Composed by Haddon Craftsmen, Inc.
Printed by Halliday
Bound by Publishers Book Bindery
HARPER & ROW, PUBLISHERS, INCORPORATED